TAKE HIM

to

Court

S A R A H   M A C K E Y

authorHOUSE®

AuthorHouse™
1663 Liberty Drive
Bloomington, IN 47403
www.authorhouse.com
Phone: 833-262-8899

Published by AuthorHouse 10/31/2022

ISBN: 978-1-6655-7477-8 (sc)
ISBN: 978-1-6655-7476-1 (e)

Print information available on the last page.

All scriptures were taken from the King James version of the Bible.

This book is printed on acid-free paper.

To my son Sidney Andrew Mackey: this one is for you. We *had* to take him to Court. Refusing to listen to the voice of that liar, we presented our case before the Righteous Judge, and He gave us total victory!

This one is for you who have lost everything, even your faith; you who think you can't break that bad habit, always falling short; you who have wandered far away from God, finding it so hard to come back to Him; you whose dreams have been squashed; you who have lost all hope because "someone" sold you a lie; and you who are experiencing disappointment after disappointment, discouragement, despair, doubt, defeat! I dedicate this book to you.

To believers everywhere: someone has stolen your authority in God, and you are having a hard time exercising complete trust in Him. Voices of "I can't …" and "I don't …" and "The doctor said …" and "My friend said …" and "My lawyer said …" and "People say …" are constantly dominating you. Wake up! You are being negatively influenced by the lies, half-truths, and misconceptions of the enemy. Someone is squatting on your land and living there for free, robbing you of everything that God has already given to you. I dedicate this book to you.

This is your season to "take him to Court" and take back everything he has stolen from you.

Contents

Author's Note

I was admonished to study the first five books of the Bible. By studying these books, I reacquainted myself with God's teachings and instructions (613 laws of God, habits that govern us). It became clear to me I was not truly following the Lord as I should; I was quoting scriptures (talking) rather than applying them to my daily life (walking). So, I repented! I changed my mindset.

Lack of knowledge (ignorance) will keep us in bondage; disobedience and rebelliousness will keep us from our blessings and inheritance. Are you going to just sit down and do nothing? It is time to get up and F-I-G-H-T! Fight for your birthright!

Remember: faith gives you the birthright (access), but obedience brings the blessings! Joshua 1:8 says, "This book of the law shall not depart out of thy mouth; but thou shalt meditate therein day and night, that thou mayest observe to do according to all that is written therein: for then thou shalt make thy way prosperous, and then thou shalt have good success."

We have been given authority on the earth; let us use our God-given authority (Luke 10:19)!

Be courageous! Take Him to Court!

Acknowledgments

To my Heavenly Father: I thank You for the knowledge gained, the understanding received, and the wisdom applied, giving me strength, boldness, and courage to stand up and fight!

To my many friends, family members, encouragers, advisors, and counselors: your collective contributions made this book possible.

Thank you, Dr. Cindy Wade (history teacher), and Ms. Donnica Dunkley (language arts teacher), for the many hours you spent editing, but apart from that, for taking the time to encourage and motivate me. I appreciate all that you have done.

Thank you, Ms. Donnica Dunkley, though you were sick and at your weakest, you were strong. Thank you for your courage; it is a testament to your character.

To my husband, Sidney: I am so grateful for your love and support. Thank you for believing in me.

To my daughter, Sara-Ashley: I went to Court many days for you. I demanded my right!

To my sons Sharif, Shaquille, Sidney Jr., and Sharad: You are my righteous seeds - the fruit of my womb that was promised blessings. The Righteous Judge understood that I knew my rights! Walk in the blessings that God has promised you. Look neither to the right nor to the left.

To my grandchildren, great-grandchildren, and great-great-grandchildren: I have already gone to Court for you; you have a Godly inheritance. This victory is for you!

To Bishop Harvey Cash: thank you for your encouragements. They were right on time and right on point.

To Dr. Maxine Evans, my sister: your counsels were wise, your rebukes were very sharp, and your encouragement was motivating. The fact that you fought alongside me—making sure I had the right scriptures, the right tone, the right feel—made this book so incredibly special. You have inspired me!

To Ursula Mackey, Yolanda Miller, Elouise McKenzie, Talitha Clarke, Tharan Brice, Kim Deveaux, Linda McDonald, Elizabeth Mills, and Deborah Gilbert: your struggles are and were real, but you represent the Kingdom well. Thank you for sharing and being there for me.

Shaquille, Sidney, Sara, Sharad, and Tonyque all can testify about the many struggles they faced. They are witnesses brave enough to take him to Court and demand their things.

I Had Enough!

"Lord, I can't take this no more! I'm sick and tired of all dis turning around and around and around! I'm sick and tired of hearing, 'No! No! No! No! No!'"

It was 6:30 a.m., the morning of September 13, 2012. The sky was draped in a gray-orange outfit, as were the clouds—all different shapes and sizes displaying the beautiful, early-morning color of the sun that had just risen.

I, on the other hand, was wearing garments of disappointments and rejections; my clothing was the color of defeat and discouragement. This was my third time going to the same appointment!

As I drove along Carmichael Road, tiredness and exhaustion took hold; the heaviness from these false garments overpowered me.

Suddenly, a sick spell of "I've had enough" came over me. All the ghosts of my past came out, haunting me! One by one, they came out with finger raised high in the air, saying, "Present." Financial difficulties, roof leaks, overheated car, stolen car, right foot injuries, sickness, pain, operations, deaths, doubt, fear, tough love … *Lies! Lies! You are all liars!*

With the little bit of energy I had left, I pulled my little green vehicle over to the side of the road and cried out to my God: "Lord, I can't take this no more! I'm sick and tired of all dis turning around and around and around! I'm sick and tired of hearing, 'No! No! No! No! No!'"

As thoughts of stealing lingered in my mind, a lion began to roar deep within my soul.

And now, after two years of trying to get a scholarship for my son Sidney, for the third time, I am given the same answer: "Nothing yet!"

* * *

SARAH: Why, Lord, why? What folly have I done? Am I not Your child? Have I not given my life over to You since I was ten years old? Haven't I obeyed You, in baptism at thirteen and surrendering my life at twenty-one? Lord, I go to church, pay my tithe. I have been serving You my whole life. What did I miss? Surely, there must be an explanation for all of this!

GOD: That's good, My child, and I applaud you, but you have rejected *Me*—knowledge. "My people are destroyed for lack of knowledge: because thou hast rejected knowledge, I will also reject thee, that thou shalt be no priest to me: seeing thou hast forgotten the law of thy God, I will also forget thy children" (Hosea 4:6).

God shakes His head.
Let Me show you disobedience and rebellion.

SARAH: I read about Adam and Eve in the Garden of Eden.

GOD, *looking squarely at me*: It's not only Adam and Eve, not only the children of Israel. It's My people; it's the church and it is you.

In Matthew 18:21–22, I say forgive "until seventy times seven." You suck your teeth and say, "He did me wrong; I am not going to forgive nor forget."

In Matthew 22:37 and 39, I say, "Love your neighbor as yourself." You won't even raise your hand or toot your horn to your neighbor.

And in Colossians 3 and Ephesians 4, I say put off the works of darkness; instead, you have put them on. And ye are clothed daily with fear and doubt and unbelief, operating under the influences of the enemy, believing his lies. For that reason, the enemy took a legal stand against you—because you will not be obedient to the Lord your God.

The Squatter

SARAH: Lord, You mean to tell me ignorance caused this?

GOD: And it wasn't just your ignorance; it was about your walk (fear, doubt, unbelief, lack of faith). It is about your bitterness and your anger and your wrath and evil speaking, with all malice. And because of this, you, your children, your grand-, great-grand-, great-great-grandchildren will pay for generations to come.

SARAH: O Lordy! O Lordy! Jesus, Savior, pilot me over life's tempestuous sea! Lord, I raise my hands to Thee; no other help I know. If Thou shalt take Thy hands from me, whether shall I go, Lord? Whether shall I go?

GOD: My child, you have been deceived! My truth has always been there for you, yet you choose to believe the lies the enemy has sold you all these years. Satan tricked you into thinking that you can do as you like and as you please. But you have been given My commands. I gave you 613 laws to govern you. You are just too lazy to study to gain knowledge! You don't love Me; you love iPhone, Android, even Bubbler. You love Facebook, WhatsApp, Twitter, PlayStation, and television. But buck your big toe, and it's "Lord, help me!" When you are sick, it's "Lord, heal me!" When you need a job, it's "Help me, Lord!"

I am weary of you putting everyone and everything else above Me. I am sick of all the grudges you are still holding on to—the bitterness, the anger, the evil speaking, the secret jealousy. How much more do you want Me to take?

You are neither hot nor cold; you make Me sick. I will spew you out of My mouth!

Sarah groans, and groans, and groans.

You don't know who you are dealing with, aye? You are not only wrestling against flesh and blood, but against principalities, against powers, against the rulers of the darkness of this world, against spiritual wickedness in high places (Ephesians 6:12). He is Satan, the Accuser of the Brethren. He accused Joshua in Zechariah 3:3, Job in Job 1:9–11. Every day, he accuses you according to Revelation 12:10.

God does not stop there …

I gave you authority on this earth; I said, "Thou shalt tread upon the lion and adder: the young lion and the dragon shalt thou trample under feet" (Psalm 91:13). But no, you are afraid of the terror by night, the arrow that flieth by day, the pestilence that walketh in darkness, and the destruction that wasteth at noonday (Psalm 91:1–7).

Why, Sarah? Why? I have not given you "the spirit of fear; but of power, and of love, and of a sound mind" (2 Timothy 1:7).

And to answer your question about you going to church and paying your tithe—that is why he is stealing right now. I take more pleasure in your obedience than you going to church, paying tithes, singing in the church choir, being on the usher board, conducting praise and worship, beating the drums, playing the piano, cleaning the church, or anything else for that matter. That's why he's been squatting. "Behold, to obey is better than sacrifice, and to hearken than the fat of rams" (1 Samuel 15:22).

The Accuser has taken a legal stand against you; he will wreak havoc on you and your children for generations to come. He is in your house right now, eating up all your food and wearing all your clothes, and driving all your cars.

SARAH, *speaking in her native dialect*: Vell mudda sick! Great dog! Wey he dere! Wey he dere!

I looked in my bedroom, I looked under my bed, I looked in my closet. When I find him, he dead! I looked around my kitchen, I looked in every pot on my stove 'cause when I find him, God only knows … O Jesus!

Sarah becomes inconsolable, sobbing.

Close every door, close every window, and close every hole, Lord! What a fool I have been all these years; I allowed fear and doubt and lack of faith to control me through ignorance.

GOD: "How long wilt thou sleep, O sluggard? When wilt thou arise out of thy sleep?" (Proverbs 6:9).

SARAH: When? When will I arise out of my sleep, Lord? I have clothespins on my eyelids right now. And whenever I do go to bed, I am going with all my clothes on. And I am keeping my hands on my sword at all times—the sword of the Spirit.

He entered my house while I was sleeping, bound me up and stole my possessions. Matthew 12:29: because he is a thief. But You said when a thief is caught, he has to repay sevenfold.

And … and You are not a man that You should lie. And … and You can't go back on Your Word.

GOD: My Word in Proverbs 6:31, Numbers 23:19, Titus 1:2, and Luke 2:23.

SARAH: Then this is not going down like this! I am calling my lawyer right now!

From this moment, I despise the enemy of my soul! I look at him with contempt (Proverbs 6:30).

Once I lay a hand on him, I will take him to Court (Matthew 12:29). He will be summoned (Exodus 22:2; Leviticus 5:16; Proverbs 6:31)!

She sucks her teeth.

False accuser! Liar! Thief! Murderer! You will not steal from me again … I am taking legal action against you.

✳   ✳   ✳

I started one piece of praying, repenting, confessing, and praising God!

Headline News ... September 13, 2012

"Her door was left wide open; anybody could enter in."

A scene erupted on Carmichael Road over someone stealing somebody's things because they thought they had the right to them. This woman went berserk after learning that for years, the enemy had been squatting on her land, living and sleeping in her house for free for forty years!

An eyewitness spoke of how this woman started one piece of praying: repenting, confessing, and praising God!

It was said that by the time she was finished, the devil and all his imps had to get out of that house as fast as they could because their lies were now exposed, and the truth was revealed. They knew they were in the wrong and did not want to have to deal with her lawyer (Jesus Christ) because she threatened to take the devil to Court to get back all her things!

They tried to escape, but it was too late! They were caught red-handed!

That day, they were arrested!

Caught Red-Handed!

The Developing Story ... September 12, 2013

This woman—a child of God and a law-abiding citizen—rolled back the curtains of her life one day and was amazed to recount how many disappointments, discouragements, depressions, delays, and debts she had encountered. And now she was told after two years, this being their third time trying to secure a scholarship for her son, "Nothing yet"!

This woman, being the good, lazy Christian she was, accepted those kind words as she always did—no questions asked (lazy and fearful). But something then happened that day: she came to her senses! Her memory was restored.

Reacting to the Word that was wedged deep within her soul, she repeated, "Is there anything too hard for God? There is nothing too hard for my God" (Jeremiah 32:27).

Her mind went all the way back to the Garden of Eden, where this same person lied to our first father, Adam. And today, he was trying that same trick, talking doubt around this woman's head: "God never came through for you before. You think God will come through now? Remember now, it's been two years, and you have already tried three times. Maybe your God is sleeping, maybe He is dead, or maybe He just does not care! Sure you are His child?"

That was when Sarah Jane Clarke Mackey from Moss Town, Exuma, put on all her "clothes" (truth, righteousness, faith, and the Word of God).

This woman had already lost her father, her sister, her brother, and her nephew. And her mother did not even know her because of Alzheimer's, with both legs amputated. She had already been rock bottom in her finances—even at death's door, experiencing the excruciating pain of loss—and now, someone was squatting on her land, stealing her things, and living there for free. The devil is a liar!

She went back to school to get wisdom, knowledge, and understanding. She was so serious about changing her mindset that she spent extra hours studying Genesis, Exodus, Leviticus, Numbers, and Deuteronomy (God's teachings and instructions for living). The scales were removed from her eyes; her ignorance, disobedience, rebelliousness, laziness, and fearfulness were exposed; and the liar, thief, and murderer was identified. His name was the Accuser of the Brethren.

All these years, she had never exercised her authority in Christ as a blood-washed believer. Because of lack of knowledge, she had allowed disobedience and rebellion to take over her house, causing her financial blessings, her success, her health, her peace, and her joy.

When she awoke out of her sleep and learned the truth of who she was and the authority she possessed as a born-again believer, she quickly acknowledged her iniquity (sins of her forefathers) and transgressions and repented of her sins. She went down to Deuteronomy 28:1 and made a vow to the Lord, her God. She went up to her thought life and cast down imaginations, and quickly cleansed her way by heeding the Word of God.

She was now determined to do the right things the right way, walking as God intended and not listening to the voice of that deceiver: the one who was cast down because of rebellion.

Today, she is warning everyone, "Beware! Beware of a thief, a liar, and murderer! Do not fall prey to his schemes."

Read more about him on the next page.

Court in The Heavens for Rebellion

Case No. 001

SATAN:

> (Satan said in his heart), I will ascend into heaven, I will exalt my throne above the stars of God: I will sit also upon the mount of the congregation, in the sides of the north: I will ascend above the heights of the clouds; I will be like the Most High. Isaiah 14:13–14:

THE RIGHTEOUS JUDGE: Yet thou art a man, and not God, though thou set thine heart as the heart of God (Isaiah 14:9–14).

"Thus saith the Lord God; Thou sealest up the sum, full of wisdom, and perfect in beauty. Thou hast been in Eden the garden of God; every precious stone was thy covering, the sardius, topaz, and the diamond, the beryl, the onyx, and the jasper, the sapphire, the emerald, and the carbuncle, and gold: the workmanship of thy tabrets and of thy pipes was prepared in thee in the day that thou wast created. Thou art the anointed cherub that covereth; and I have set thee so: thou wast upon the holy mountain of God; thou hast walked up and down in the midst of the stones of fire. Thou wast perfect in thy ways from the day that thou wast created, till iniquity was found in thee. By the multitude of thy merchandise, they have filled the midst of thee with violence, and thou hast sinned: therefore I will cast thee as profane out of the mountain of God: and I will destroy thee, O covering cherub, from the midst of the stones of fire. ... Thou hast defiled thy sanctuaries by the multitude of thine iniquities, by the iniquity of thy traffick; therefore will I bring forth a fire from the midst of thee, it shall devour thee, and I will bring thee to ashes upon the earth in the sight of all them that behold thee." Ezekiel 28:12–16, 18.

You have been cast down to the earth, you who once laid low the nations! Morning star, son of the dawn, how art thou fallen from heaven? O Lucifer, son of the morning, how art thou cut down to the ground, which didst weaken the nations?

You are brought down to the realm of the dead, to the depths of the pit. Thou shalt die the deaths of the uncircumcised by the hand of strangers.

I have spoken it, saith the Lord God (Ezekiel 2–10).

Court in The Garden for Deception

Case No. 002

Genesis 3:1–14, 17:

Now the serpent was more subtle than any beast of the field which the Lord God had made. And he said unto the woman, Yea, hath God said, Ye shall not eat of every tree of the garden?

And the woman said unto the serpent, We may eat of the fruit of the trees of the garden: But of the fruit of the tree which is in the midst of the garden, God hath said, Ye shall not eat of it, neither shall ye touch it, lest ye die.

And the serpent said unto the woman, Ye shall not surely die: For God doth know that in the day ye eat thereof, then your eyes shall be opened, and ye shall be as gods, knowing good and evil.

And when the woman saw that the tree was good for food, and that it was pleasant to the eyes, and a tree to be desired to make one wise, she took of the fruit thereof, and did eat, and gave also unto her husband with her; and he did eat.

And the eyes of them both were opened, and they knew that they were naked; and they sewed fig leaves together, and made themselves aprons.

And they heard the voice of the Lord God walking in the garden in the cool of the day: and Adam and his wife hid themselves from the presence of the Lord God amongst the trees of the garden.

And the Lord God called unto Adam, and said unto him, Where art thou?

And he said, I heard thy voice in the garden, and I was afraid, because I was naked; and I hid myself.

And he said, Who told thee that thou wast naked? Hast thou eaten of the tree, whereof I commanded thee that thou shouldest not eat?

And the man said, The woman whom thou gavest to be with me, she gave me of the tree, and I did eat.

And the Lord God said unto the woman, What is this that thou hast done?

And the woman said, The serpent beguiled me, and I did eat.

And the Lord God said unto the serpent, Because thou hast done this, Thou art cursed above all cattle, And above every beast of the field; Upon thy belly shalt thou go, And dust shalt thou eat all the days of thy life …

Sarah Mackey

And unto Adam he said, Because thou hast hearkened unto the voice of thy wife, and hast eaten of the tree, of which I commanded thee, saying, Thou shalt not eat of it: cursed is the ground for thy sake; in sorrow shalt thou eat of it all the days of thy life.

Court in My Closet

Case No. 003

SARAH: The Lord spoke to my heart that day and said, "Like Adam and Eve, you've been given My commands and you've despised and rejected them."

Falling down on my knees before God, I said, "Lord … O Lord, please forgive me! I ask Your forgiveness and pardon for all the years I've ignorantly with all stupidity defied the God of heaven and earth. I have been disobedient to my Lord, my Savior, and my Master. I have done You shamefully wrong! I have turned my back on knowledge and understanding and wisdom.

"O Father, please forgive me for all the years I lived this rebellious and disobedient lifestyle. I said I loved You, but I was only giving You lip service; I have been confessing to You with my mouth. But my heart was far from You; my heart was far from walking according to Your teachings and instructions.

"I allowed the Accuser of the Brethren, Satan, to enter my house because my whole life was filled with doubts and fears and unbelief. Lord, You were not on my throne. Because of my disobedience, I gave Satan rights to steal my possessions, take my authority, squat on my land, and live there for free.

"Lord, I confess my lack of knowledge—ignorance. Right now, Lord, I confess my laziness. I confess my doubts, fears, and unbelief right now! I confess my iniquities and transgressions, and I confess the sins and iniquities of my forefathers (knowingly and unknowingly): idolatry, covetousness, adultery, deception, murder, theft, and lies.

"Jesus, Savior, pilot me! Look what ignorance did to me. Look at my disobedience. See how I rebelled, Lord. Look at the one I listened to, whom You sentenced to hell …"

I cried even louder! "O Lord, search my heart, search my mind; destroy all the lawlessness and rebelliousness You can find. Purify, purge, and repattern me from within. Remove all the filth, the garbage, the sin. Forgive my ignorance; I really did not know, but now, disobedience and rebellion, they *have* to go! Forgive my laziness, forgive my fear; I no longer want them living with me in here!

"O Lord, have mercy upon me. Give me another chance. I will start all over and begin with Your standards, Your laws, and Your commands. Blot out my transgressions and cleanse me from my sins; allow me to adjust to Your loving kindness and tender mercies from deep within.

"I yield to You, O Lord. To fear I will no longer bow, because now, I will fear You with all my heart and with all my soul, with my entire mind and with all my strength. This I vow in Jesus's name. Amen!"

Functioning in Court

Case No. 003 Continues

SARAH: I read somewhere where it is said, "If you are going to meet God, it must be at a special place, and at a special time, for He is a Special Person. That's when God functions in Court, the three-hour increment times: nine, twelve, three, and six." With that knowledge, I became profoundly serious because now, this was my special time to go to Court to meet this Special Person at my special place: His Court (my closet).

I gathered myself and became very still, bringing my spirit, body, mind, and emotions into unity with God so that I could pray God's will with singleness of purpose.

As I entered my closet (Courtroom) to pray, I said, "Lord, I understand that Your name gives You power, and that You need me to speak it because I have been given authority, God, that You take Your power through my authority, which is Your Word.

"Father, You said to just say Your words and You will sort it out for me. Lord, You ask me, Your child, to come into Your chambers and You will give me Judge's privileges on behalf of my children and my children's children."

With hands lifted high, heart, mind, and soul in oneness, I worshipped! "O Elohim, You alone are the Creator, El Elyon- You are the Most High God. You are the God who sees everything. El Roi,

You are my Shepherd, and I shall not want—my El Shaddai, my All-Sufficient One.

"Adonai, Lord, You sit on the throne, worthy to be praised! You are my Master, and I am Your slave. Jehovah Raah, You are my healer. You have healed me before the foundation of the world; You provided for me when I did not know when, where, nor how, Jehovah-Jireh.

"Thank You, Jehovah-Nissi, my banner and my battle-ax. You have given me victory in every area of my life and the peace that passeth all understanding, Jehovah Shalom. Today, YAHWEH, You are My Saving Justice!

"The book of Revelation tells me that You are the Alpha and Omega, the First and the Last, the Beginning and the End—the Almighty! You are the Lion of the Tribe of Judah, King of Kings and Lord of Lords! There is none like You in heaven above nor the earth beneath nor under the seas. You alone are able to do exceedingly, abundantly above all that I ask or think.

O Lord, "hear the prayer of thy servant, and her supplications, according to (Daniel 9:17-19) and cause thy face to shine upon thy sanctuary that is desolate, for the Lord's sake. O my God, incline thine ear, and hear; open thine eyes … for I do not present my supplications before thee for my righteousnesses, but for thy great mercies. O Lord, hear; O Lord, forgive; O Lord, hearken and do; defer not, for thine own sake, O my God.'

"Have mercy upon me, O God, according to thy word in (Psalms 51:1-4) according to thy loving kindness: according unto the multitude of thy tender mercies blot out my transgressions. Wash me thoroughly from mine iniquity, and cleanse me from my sin. For I acknowledge my transgressions: and my sin is ever before me. Against thee, thee only, have I sinned, and done this evil in thy sight: that thou mightest be justified when thou speakest, and be clear when thou judgest. For thou desirest not sacrifice; else would I give it: thou delightest not in burnt offering. The sacrifices of God are a broken spirit: a broken and a contrite heart, O God, thou wilt not despise.'

"Lord, after reading Your 613 principles, I am here present today to agree with You. What You say about me—it is all true. O Lord God, I have sinned and done You wrong, and I ask for forgiveness and pardon for all the years I ignorantly defied the God of heaven as I bring my case to prayer (Court).

"Plead my cause and redeem me; revive me according to Your Word. O Lord, revive me according to Your justice in Yeshua's name. Amen!"

I was not leaving any doors open anymore! I know who I am.

I Know Who I Am

- I am a seed of Abraham, Isaac, and Jacob (Galatians 3:29).
- I am the righteousness of God in Jesus Christ (2 Corinthians 5:21).
- I am delivered from the power of darkness (Colossians 1:13).
- I am redeemed from the curse of sin, sickness, and poverty (Deuteronomy 28:15–68; Galatians 3:13), for God has given us a spirit not of fear but of power, love, and a sound mind (2 Timothy 1:7).
- I am more than a conqueror through Him who loves me (Romans 8:37).
- I have power over all the power of the enemy (Luke 10:17, 19).
- I am of a royal priesthood (1 Peter 2:9).
- I am a holy nation (1 Peter 2:9).
- I am the apple of His eye (Deuteronomy 32:10).
- I am the head and not the tail (Deuteronomy 28:13).
- I am above only and not beneath (Deuteronomy 28:13).
- I can do all things through Christ who strengthens me (Philippians 4:13).

This time, I know my legal rights! This time, he is messing with the right woman the wrong time! This time, she has learned how to come in to God and come back to Him the right way!

Thank You, Lord! Thank You, Jesus! Thank You for showing me mercy!

Who is a God like You, who pardons sin and forgives the transgression of the remnant of His inheritance? You do not stay angry forever but delight to show mercy (Micah 7:18).

Thank You, Lord! Thank You, Jesus! Thank You for forgiving my transgressions and my sins! You all are worthy to receive all the glory! All the honor! All the power and all the praise!

Accused

Case No. 004

Accuser of the Brethren v. Sarah

(God the Righteous Judge presiding)
Transcript of Sarah Jane Mackey
Date of birth: May 4, 1972
Accused of: Disobedience, rebelliousness, lack of knowledge, lack of faith, fearfulness, and laziness

*   *   *

Court was already in session by the time Sarah understood her rights.

THE RIGHTEOUS JUDGE: Satan, where have you come from?

ACCUSER OF THE BRETHREN: From roaming about on the earth and walking around on it, and from squatting in Sarah's house. All day long, she leaves her doors open! Anybody could come in!

Look at her; she has Your Word for wisdom, knowledge, and understanding, and she is despising it. Just look at how she treats her birthright; she acts as if it means nothing to her, and I am talking about every single day!

You have given her authority over me; instead, she is in fear of me. What kind of children have You produced? As simple as it is to obey Your Word, Your Voice, she cannot even do that. That's downright rebellious! Why are You tolerating her? Are You going to let her get away with this? Are You going to just sit there and let this child of Yours consistently disobey You and rebel against You?

You are God, a God of order! I know she will come crying to You about "she didn't know." Nonsense! Ignorance is not an excuse!

You are God. Judge her! Judge this lazy, fearful, ignorant, disobedient, and rebellious—

Suddenly, heaven's Courtroom door burst open! Sarah had finally learned how to take legal action against this thief, liar, and murderer.

Know Your Rights

As a believer in Christ, you are now joint heir with Christ.

You are the righteousness of God.

You have legal rights as a child of God.

Your adoption gives you privileges.

You have the right to be a part of the family of God.

You have God's favor.

You are no longer a slave but free; whoever the Son sets free is free indeed.

Royal blood runs through your veins; exercise your authority.

You are a holy nation; govern yourself accordingly.

You are sanctified, redeemed. Your sins are atoned for; walk in your calling.

You have the right to ask, and it shall be given.

You have the right to call. Before you call, God will answer; while you are yet speaking, He will hear.

You have the right to say to that mountain, "Be thou removed."

You have the right to be healed; by His stripes, you are healed.

You have the right to prosper.

You have the right to be in good health.

You have the right to joy and peace.

You have the right to never fear again; God did not give that to us.

You have the right to power, love, and a sound mind; exercise your authority.

You have the right to the peace that passeth all understanding; spend time praising God.

You have the right to pray in the Name of Jesus; every demon must flee. After every battle, you have the right to victory.

You have the right to resist the devil, and he will flee from you. You have the right to take him to Court.

Inheritance Rediscoved

This time, she learned the facts about her inheritance.

SARAH: The Kingdom of God is within me (His laws and precepts)!

That is my inheritance! It is an inheritance to a perfect righteousness that allows me to stand before God uncondemned! I can stand against every devil and demon in hell because principles defeat principalities. Satan will not be able to accuse me before God, my Father, before my brethren—even before my own conscience—because I am an heir, an heir to the perfect righteousness of Jesus Christ!

Lord, I thought that my discouragements, distresses, disappointments, and debts were normal. I let that devil strip me of my joy, my peace, my love for God. I was so ignorant; I did not know how to use my authority in God, being disobedient to God's teachings and instructions.

For years, he had me thinking that my current financial situation was God's plan for me … and also that I had to stop Sidney from going to college for a semester. Lies! Lies! Liar! The devil is a liar!

And the rest of my blessings are in the "treasures of darkness" hoarded by the devil and his imps: my financial blessings, my talent, my children's blessings, my books not written, my deliverance!

I am not letting this go like this! I will not let you jump slick on me again! Not today, Devil! I am going to take legal actions against you! Today, I am taking you to Court!

I've arrived right on time to catch that liar! The Accuser of the Brethren, Satan, is already before the Righteous Judge, accusing me.

Sarah Mackey

In Contempt of Court

SARAH, *bursting into Court*: You liar! Teef! Murderer! You have been teefing all my things, selling me lies, and living for free all these years. I will not let you get away with this! You tink I'm still ignorant! Not anymore! I know about your schemes and tricks ... You tried that with Eve and Adam, but not with me this time—not today!

THE RIGHTEOUS JUDGE, *whispering*: Michael, Michael, that's My child! See how fearless she has become? She came into My Court with boldness. Now how can I hold her in contempt of Court? She is on time; she knows her rights, and she ain't scared. *That's My child!*

Sarah, I will not tolerate any more lawlessness (fear, doubt, unbelief) in My Court!

SARAH: Father, when I found out the *truth*, I could not contain myself.

THE RIGHTEOUS JUDGE: Don't you know that "My people are destroyed for lack of knowledge" (Hosea 4:6)? You have allowed fear, doubt, and unbelief to be the open door for the enemy to steal from you. As a matter of fact, he has filed another one of his complaints against you. He is in the Court right now! But I dare him!

I Stand Accused

Case No. 004 Continues

Accuser of the Brethren v. Sarah continues …

THE RIGHTEOUS JUDGE: Continue, Accuser of the Brethren. Go ahead and accuse My child, My good child.

ACCUSER OF THE BRETHREN: Righteous Judge, as I was saying, Sarah Jane Mackey is an ignorant, disobedient, and rebellious child. I will show where her ignorance and fear were the open doors that gave me legal rights to her blessings and inheritance of the third and fourth generations.

DEFENSE ATTORNEY (THE HOLY SPIRIT): Your Honor, Satan was roaming the earth and walking up and down in it. I have the date and time when my child voluntarily submitted herself to me; repented of her disobedience and rebellion, fear, doubt, laziness, and ignorance; and confessed Your Word. I was there when she confessed and began her new life walking in the commands of God.

Righteous Judge, April 21–24, 2010, was the turning point in my child's life. September 13, 2012, was the day she understood and accepted God's teachings and instructions. And January 25, 2016, she truly began to walk. February 10, 2016, was a true picture of trust.

I remember when Sidney got a letter from college about his overdue tuition, which was cause for her to worry and fret, Righteous Judge. But Your child braved this giant, and fear went mad out the door. She had changed from lazy to searching, from doubtful to faithful, from fearful to courageous, from disobedient to obedient, and from rebellious to meek and humble.

ACCUSER OF THE BRETHREN: Righteous Judge, every idle word, every act of disobedience and rebellion, everything this weakling did are all on record. This ignorant child sold her birthright, sold her blessings, sold her inheritance and her children's and her children's children's with one simple act ... disobedience.

DEFENSE ATTORNEY (THE HOLY SPIRIT): Righteous Judge, yes, Your Word clearly states in Hosea 4:6, "My people are destroyed for lack of knowledge." *But* it also states in 2 Chronicles 7:14, "If my people, which are called by my name, shall humble themselves, and pray, and seek my face, and turn from their wicked ways; then will I hear from heaven, and will forgive their sin, and will heal their land."

THE RIGHTEOUS JUDGE: My Word indeed! Overruled!

ACCUSER OF THE BRETHREN: Okay den! Okay den! All these curses will come on you. They will pursue you and overtake you until you are destroyed, because you did not obey the Lord your God, and observe the commands and decrees He gave you. They will be a sign and a wonder to you and your descendants forever. Because you did not serve the Lord your God joyfully and gladly in the time of prosperity, therefore in hunger and thirst, in nakedness and dire poverty, you will serve the enemies the Lord sends against you. He will put an iron yoke on your neck until he has destroyed you.

Your words, Righteous Judge?

DEFENSE ATTORNEY (THE HOLY SPIRIT): My child has already repented.

ACCUSER OF THE BRETHREN: Objection! Repentance—too late! God's Word stands sure!

DEFENSE ATTORNEY (THE HOLY SPIRIT): For sure, Accuser! 2 Chronicles 6:37 (NIV)—"If they have a change of heart in the land where they are held captive, and repent and plead with you in the land of their captivity and say, 'We have sinned, we have done wrong and acted wickedly.'"

The Holy Spirit looked directly at the Accuser of the Brethren.
Something Satan does not know how to do—he does not submit to authority. You are rebellious, proud, and arrogant!

ACCUSER OF THE BRETHREN: I will pretend I did not hear that. By the way, where was I when all this happened? I need to see those transcripts.

DEFENSE ATTORNEY (THE HOLY SPIRIT): That proves my point: only YAHWEH is everywhere (omnipresent), only YAHWEH has all power (omnipotent), and only YAHWEH knows everything (omniscient)!

The Holy Spirit then turned to the jury and witnesses.
This is why my children need to apply Joshua 1:8, Psalm 91, Psalm 121, and Proverbs 3:5–6 to their daily living; in all your ways, acknowledge YAHWEH.

ACCUSER OF THE BRETHREN: He-he-he! You won that one.

Feeling humiliated, he hurriedly went on.

Well then, I take legal action against her disobedience and rebellion. See her there, she's just like her mother Eve. Remember how cunning I was to get Eve to disobey Your commands? You told Sarah You gave her power, love, and a sound mind; but instead, she chooses the spirit of fear.

Even I believe! Ignorant child!

You told her to love You with all her heart, but instead, she only gives you half, if that. You told her about Psalm 91, and You told her about Psalm 121, which she quotes almost every single day. But, does she believe You? Just talking, talking, talking—no walking, walking, walking.

Boy, genes don't lie. Sarah ain't no different ... just downright disobedient! You gave this human being everything she needed, yet she rebelled, after all You have done for her!

According to Leviticus 26:16, and I quote, "And ye shall sow your seed in vain, for your enemies shall eat it." I am that enemy, Righteous Judge; You gave me the right to her possessions because of disobedience. I demand my right!

DEFENSE ATTORNEY (THE HOLY SPIRIT): But Righteous Judge, again, Leviticus 26:3, 7 and Deuteronomy 28:1, 7 clearly state, "If ye walk in my statutes, and keep my commandments, and do them ... ye shall chase your enemies, and they shall fall before you by the sword."

"And it shall come to pass, if thou shalt hearken diligently unto the voice of the Lord thy God, to observe and to do all his commandments which I command thee this day, that the Lord thy God will set thee on high above all nations of the earth ... The Lord shall cause thine enemies that rise up against thee to be smitten before thy face: they shall come out against thee one way, and flee before thee seven ways."

ACCUSER OF THE BRETHREN: I object!

DEFENSE ATTORNEY (THE HOLY SPIRIT): Object? You cannot object to YAHWEH'S Word; you cannot object to truth! You are a liar, a thief, and a murderer! You will soon have your day in hell!

ACCUSER OF THE BRETHREN: That's why I am like a roaring lion, seeking whom I may devour. That's why I will continue to take these disobedient and rebellious children to Court; I want to keep many from serving You—to keep them blind, fearful, and ignorant!

Righteous Judge, for years, Mrs. Mackey spent hours and hours and hours watching television needlessly, talking on the phone endlessly, and doing everything else carelessly, never taking time out to study Your Word. She has a bad attitude, thinking she already knows everything by the little bit of scriptures she learned. She is full of pride and empty of wisdom, knowledge, and understanding. Look here … she thinks she's so spiritual.

DEFENSE ATTORNEY (THE HOLY SPIRIT): I was there with her at the tender age of ten in her father's old truck in Moss Town, Exuma, when Sarah accepted me as Lord and Savior. I was there at the Big Hill Beach when, at thirteen, she was baptized according to my commands. I was there at twenty-one on Jerome Avenue when she rededicated her life to me. But most recently and significantly, I was there on April 21, 2010, when she applied Deuteronomy 28:1. Again, where were you?

ACCUSER OF THE BRETHREN, *sucking his teeth*: But for the last forty years, I have been able to deceive this child of Yours to trust what her eyes saw. Let me show You disobedience through fear.

- Remember when her husband lost all his contracts with his company? You were there. You said, "Trust in the Lord with all thine heart." Her eyes were not on You; she was looking to everybody but You.
- I almost nailed her down when she had that accident; that was the worst. He-he! She almost lost her mind through fear. She had panic attacks for months. You said, "I have given you the spirit not of fear, but of power and a sound mind." Fearful child.
- How about the time with Shaquille—you know what I'm talking about? What about the time when Sharad went off to college all by himself? You were there. I had her; she was worried sick. I had her in a deep depression. Need I go on?
- But I must give her this one: when she took Ashley to college and was told she needed $3,500. I thought I had her, being in a faraway country with no one to call on; but this girl exercised some crazy faith. Next thing I knew, she had $3,000. She was bold and fearless!

But still this spirit body trusts me more than she trusts You and she has Your Word—Righteous Judge, Your Word. She only talks faith; she surely does not know how to fully walk. Someone needs to teach her.

I take a legal stand against her fear. She does not deserve what You have for her; she is too scared to stand up and fight for her things which truly belong to her! Ignorant, lazy, and fearful Christian!

A Holy God does not tolerate disobedience or rebelliousness. Ask Aaron and his sons Nadab and Abihu (the priests). Ask Saul. Ask Moses.

Ask Satan; that is me. I was kicked out of heaven. I learned the hard way. Sorry, I never learn; I will continue to kill, steal and destroy as many, y'all sleep on me.

Sarah Jane, I put it to you that you did not obey; you only did it halfway. God said, "I wish that you were either hot or cold." You said, "Lukewarm." You make God sick!

Hebrews 11:6 says, "But without faith it is impossible to please him: for he that cometh to God must believe that he is, and that he is a rewarder of them that diligently seek him."

Righteous Judge, based on subsection 3 of Your Word, she walks in doubt and lives every day in fear; she does not trust You with all her heart. You see, Righteous Judge, faith is built on trust, and trust is built on relationship, and a relationship is between two people.

I can assuredly say that I had a relationship with Sarah Jane Mackey because she was always listening to my voice: fear, doubt, and depression, discouragement, debt, delay, defeat. Need I go on?

As a matter of fact, I can confidently say she has confidence in You, but ... but she lacks persistence. She trusts me more than she trusts *You* ... He-he-he!

DEFENSE ATTORNEY (THE HOLY SPIRIT): Righteous Judge, Satan is taunting Your child!

ACCUSER OF THE BRETHREN: He-he-he! I rest, Righteous Judge; I rest. He-he-he-he-he-he!

THE RIGHTEOUS JUDGE: Call the accused.

For just a moment, still in her old mindset, forgetting who she was, Sarah started again.

SARAH: Jesus Savior, pilot me over life's tempestuous seas; unknown ways before me roll. Lord, I raise my hands to Thee. No other help I know. If thou would take thine hand from me, whither should I go? O Lamb of God of Calvary ...

This was much to the displeasure of the Judge. Suddenly, Sarah heard the crash of the gavel!

THE RIGHTEOUS JUDGE: Why isn't My child using her God-given authority? My child will be destroyed if she does not stand up and fight.

Court is in recess for fifteen minutes to give the accused time to recollect herself.

No Witnesses

BAILIFF (Michael the Archangel): All rise! God, the Righteous Judge, is in His chambers.

THE RIGHTEOUS JUDGE: Proceed.

DEFENSE ATTORNEY (THE HOLY SPIRIT): I want to begin by apologizing for the behavior of my child. Satan, the devil, this false accuser, did not follow the protocol of this Court, and for that reason, Your child was not prepared fully for this case.

THE RIGHTEOUS JUDGE: That is no excuse! Have you ever seen Satan play it fair? He is a liar and the father of it. He is a thief and a murderer! I will not accept fearfulness and disobedience; I will not accept rebellion in My Court!

Accuser of the Brethren, call your first witness.

ACCUSER OF THE BRETHREN: I have no witnesses, Righteous Judge.

THE RIGHTEOUS JUDGE: *You have no witnesses?* You come in My Court to accuse My child, and *you have no witnesses?*

Arrest of The Accuser

THE RIGHTEOUS JUDGE: *Rebellious!* That is what I call you. An Accuser of the Brethren! You know My Word, which states, "In the mouth of two or three witnesses …" But your rebelliousness always gets the better of you.

Michael, arrest this tyrant and charge him with contempt of Court, and let him answer to the current charges brought against him by My child. She is here. Besides, we have a warrant for his arrest.

DEFENSE ATTORNEY (THE HOLY SPIRIT): This is the transcript of Satan, Lucifer, the devil, Accuser of the Brethren.

Date of birth of rebellion: Isaiah 14:14
Accused of:

- Forty years of armed robbery
- Forty years of false pretense
- Causing bodily harm to Sarah's child: right toe break with an eight-inch block, sprained right ankle, busted right shank, right foot injury with a pickax; also, the three surgeries

- The deaths of Virginia Clarke, Brendalee Taylor, and Sean Evans (Sarah might as well accuse him of the deaths of her mother, father, brother, uncle, aunty, and cousins.)

Date of arrest: September 12, 2013

Evidence

THE RIGHTEOUS JUDGE: Call the defendant.

BAILIFF (Michael the Archangel): State your name and where you live, please.

SARAH: Sarah Jane Clarke Mackey. New Providence, Bahamas.

BAILIFF (Michael the Archangel): Will you speak the truth, the whole truth, and nothing but the truth?

SARAH: I will, so help me God.

THE RIGHTEOUS JUDGE, *whispering to Michael the Archangel*: It is so refreshing to see My child operating under a sound mind and taking her authority back. Tell Gabriel to prepare for a grand celebration; make sure the praise and worship are assembled with the trumpeters and the harpers.

I understand you have brought a case against the Accuser of the Brethren? Present your case, My dear child.

SARAH: Thank You, Lord. Thank You, Jesus. Thank You, Lord. Hallelujah! Thank You for this opportunity. I can still recall the moment, dressed in a spaghetti-strap yellow popcorn blouse and yellow pants. I was sitting in my father's old broken-down truck; after reading a chick publication, I invited Jesus Christ into my heart to be my Lord and Savior. I was ten years old.

At the age of thirteen, I followed the Lord in water baptism by my late pastor, Rev. Maurice Clarke, my uncle (God rest his soul). All to Jesus I surrendered at twenty-one, and Father—

ACCUSER OF THE BRETHREN: Man, we know about all that. Get to the point, please. Talk about your walk. I don't have all day; I have plans (to kill, steal, and destroy many).

SARAH: Father, You said to come boldly before Your throne to obtain mercy and to find grace to help in the time of need. You said, "Come unto me, all ye that labour and are heavy laden, and I will give you rest" (Matthew 11:28). You said, "Ask and it shall be given; anything I ask in faith believing, I shall receive." You said, "I am the Lord, the God of all flesh: is there any thing too hard for me?" (Jeremiah 32:27). You said, "I know the plans I have for you … to give me an expected end." You said, "But without faith it is impossible to please him: for he that cometh to God must believe that he is God, and that he is a rewarder of them that diligently seek him" (Hebrews 11:6).

ACCUSER OF THE BRETHREN: Aren't you tired of using the Word? "You say! You say!"

The Rights to My Blessings

SARAH: O Abba Father, I submit myself unto Thee. This book of the law shall not depart out of my mouth; but I will meditate therein day and night. I may observe to do according to all that is written therein. For then, I will make my way prosperous, and then I will have good success.

I have repented, submitted, and committed myself to Your will and to Your way. As I, Your child, go to this appointment with the minister, I am thanking You right now for victory! I know that You are able to do exceedingly, abundantly above what I ask or think. I will not walk in doubt and fear and unbelief. I believe You and Your Word. Thank You! You said, "Before I call, you have already answered." Thank You, Jesus! Thank You for winning the case for me in Jesus's name.

Cause my enemies that rise up against me to be smitten before my face. They came out against me one way; let them flee before me seven ways.

He tried to steal Your Kingdom. He deceived Eve, my mother, and now he is here trying to steal my inheritance. He is the illegal one, deceitful in the Garden, talking about, "Did God say …?" questioning Your authority (Genesis 3:1; James 7:7; Revelation 12:9).

He is a liar, a thief, and a murderer and the Accuser of the Brethren (John 10:10; Revelation 12:1).

He corrupts the minds of believers (2 Corinthians 11:3).

He steals the Word of God from the heart (Mark 4:15).

He was rebellious from the time he was the covering cherub: "I will be like the Most High" (Ezekiel 28:12–15; James 4:7; Revelation 12:9).

Take Satan to Court

Case No. 005

Sarah v. the Accuser of the Brethren

This is the moment I was waiting for: taking Satan to Court. This is my moment in time! I'm sick and tired of his lies.

BAILIFF (Michael the Archangel): All rise, please! God the Righteous Judge presiding.

THE RIGHTEOUS JUDGE: Call the defendant.

BAILIFF (Michael the Archangel): I call Satan. Repeat after me: "I solemnly swear to tell the truth, the whole truth, and nothing but the truth; so help me God."

SATAN, *mumbling under his breath*: I cannot promise that.

BAILIFF (Michael the Archangel): Please state your name.

SATAN: Angel of Light, Lucifer, Accuser, Deceiver, Murderer, Accuser of the Brethren.

BAILIFF (Michael the Archangel): State where you reside.

SATAN: Walking up and down on the earth.

BAILIFF (Michael the Archangel): State what you do for a living.

SATAN: Seek whom I could devour. And I take delight in accusing those who are saved and have been forgiven. I corrupt the minds of believers. I steal the Word of God from the heart.

Suddenly, praise and worship broke out in the Courtroom!

SARAH: O Elohim, Adonai, You always existed! You stretched out the heavens, laid the foundations of the earth, and formed the seas. It was You and You alone! You are God the Creator who called all the stars by name and knows the number of sands on the seashore! Only You! The sun, moon, and stars rise and set at Your bidding. You are forever faithful and loving, showing mercy upon mercy to Your children.

O God, my Father, in my ignorance through rebellion and disobedience, my stupidity has landed me in a place of drought, lack, and darkness. I opened all my doors for the evil one and his imps to come in and take up residence in Your tabernacle, Your house.

I recognize my sins and iniquities. I am here today for forgiveness and pardon. I turned my back on Your Word and went the way of the world. I forsook Your teachings and instructions and listened to the voice of lawlessness from the lawless one.

Father, I confess, repent, and ask Your forgiveness on behalf of myself, my children, my children's children; for the third and fourth generations of my ancestors, and their sin and iniquity, I need Your mercy today. Thank You for Your righteous justice!

I vow to love You with all my heart and mind and soul and strength. You are so worthy to be praised, honored, and adored.

SATAN: I object!

THE HOLY SPIRIT: You are objecting to what?

SATAN, *snarling*: This is a Court of law, not a place of prayer!

THE HOLY SPIRIT: Get thee behind me, Satan. Let me remind you, Satan, prayer is coming to Court. Every child of God should know their rights—know when to take you to Court!

THE RIGHTEOUS JUDGE: Overruled! Continue, My child.

SARAH: Righteous Judge, I agree with You about what You said about me. It was through my rebellion and disobedience to Your 613 principles that I was scattered to the nations: Deuteronomy 27, 28, 20, 30. Please forgive me. Forgive my ignorance, I pray Thee; I allowed my heart to believe the lies of the enemy, destroying my faith and trust in You. Through ignorance, I left my doors open, giving the enemy legal rights. O how stupid! O how sorry I am!

I have agreed to be obedient to Your Word. I have come into agreement with You according to the words You spoke in Deuteronomy 28:1–14 and Leviticus 26:1–13.

I humbly remind you of Your Word: "If my people, which are called by my name, shall humble themselves, and pray … and turn from their wicked ways; then will I hear from heaven, and will forgive their sin, and will heal their land."

THE RIGHTEOUS JUDGE: My Word—2 Chronicles 7:14.

SARAH: O Righteous Judge, if I could but indulge You just a moment more to remind You of Your Word.

THE RIGHTEOUS JUDGE: That is what I like to hear!

SARAH: You said, "If they shall confess their iniquity, and the iniquity of their fathers, with their trespass which they trespassed against me, and that also they have walked contrary unto me; and that I also have walked contrary unto them, and have brought them into the land of their enemies" (Leviticus 26:40–41).

THE RIGHTEOUS JUDGE: I will hasten my Word to perform it.

SARAH: Today, Righteous Judge, I stand before You accused of being ignorant, disobedient, rebellious, lazy, and fearful. I confess that was me. I stand before You accused of lying about my name—that I am not a child of God, that I stole my royal identity. But who sold me the lies? Who stole from me? Who killed me all the day long?

But I will admit to this, Righteous Judge: I had always put You equal with Satan, in the end giving him more power and respect than You. I will also admit to this, Righteous Judge: I was too scared to challenge this evil force who forced me through the many fears I encountered in my life.

I confess, Righteous Judge, that for years, I did not trust You with all my heart. But on September 13, 2012, I came face-to-face with my fears, the giants in my life. I said to myself going to the minister for one last meeting, "Enough is enough! That devil is a liar!"

This devil has been lying to me and stealing all my things for the last forty years; I've had enough! He tried to steal my peace of mind, my man, and my money. I want it all back. He tried to kill me, my son, my dreams, and my plans. I want them all back. He tried to destroy my faith by replacing it with fears. I want my faith back, Lord.

I want today to be the last day he steals from me. Today, I put an end to my ignorance, disobedience, rebellion, laziness, and fear. I came kneeling to You, Your Honor, for forgiveness and cleansing. You loved me and died for me before the foundation of the world; You redeemed me, restored me, resurrected me, revived me, remembered me when everybody else was walking all over me.

My accuser standing here today accusing me is the real Accuser of the Brethren; he is the liar, the thief, and the murderer. I am present in Court today to get justice, just like that woman in Luke 18, Righteous Judge.

THE RIGHTEOUS JUDGE: Michael, call Sarah's witnesses.

BAILIFF (Michael the Archangel): The Court calls:

- Dr. Maxine Evans
- Yolanda Miller
- Ursula Mackey
- Elouise McKenzie
- Talitha Clarke
- Tharan Brice
- Kim Deveaux
- Tonyque Mackey
- Elizabeth Mills
- Tina Cunningham
- Debbie Gilbert
- Sidney Mackey
- Shaquille, Sidney Jr., Sara-Ashley, and Sharad

SARAH: They all can testify to this fact. These are witnesses brave enough to take him to Court and demand their things.

SATAN: Are these all the witnesses you have?

SARAH: Lord, you said "in the mouth of two or three"; I brought twelve plus four. I also brought case laws, Righteous Judge.

THE RIGHTEOUS JUDGE: Present your case laws, my dear child.

SARAH:

- The woman with the issue of blood struggled for twelve years, and one day, she got it; she applied Your teachings and instructions. She touched the Torah, Lord, and when she did, healing took place; deliverance took place. The blood stained her, but the blood cleaned her (Luke 8:40–56).
- Joseph was hated by his brothers, lied upon and wrongfully thrown into prison. But he had God's teachings and instructions. Because of the Torah in his life, he was able to behave himself wisely even in bonds, chained. Righteous Judge, You delivered him. You raised him from prison to the palace (Genesis 37:1–36).
- Righteous Judge, Job lost everything: children, home, land, money. He was stripped naked. But being consumed by Your teachings and instructions, his words were "God, though you slay me, yet will I trust you." Honor, You restored him double because of his obedience (Job 1:1–22, 13:15).
- Lazarus died from his sickness; he was bound with grave clothes, buried and stinking, but because of the Torah in his life, he was able to hear, "Lazarus, come forth" (John 11:1–46).

Furthermore, Lord, You pardoned:

- Ahab in 1 Kings 21:27
- Josiah in 2 Kings 22:19
- Israel in Ezra's time in Ezekiel 10:1
- Peter and the prodigal son

There is none like You, Lord! Thank You, Lord, that today I am believing You for this scholarship for Sidney. I know You will turn this situation around for Your child. I thank You for winning this case for me before the foundation of the world, Elohim, God the Creator.

Though I was lied to and stolen from, You have given me rights and a way out for me to get my things back, as is set forth in Deuteronomy 28:1 and Leviticus 26.

THE RIGHTEOUS JUDGE: I've heard enough.

Court is in recess.

It's in The Praise!

BAILIFF (Michael the Archangel): All rise!

Once the Judge went into His chambers, the jury, made up of twelve people for God's government, was in recess.
All of a sudden, praise broke out.

SARAH: Thank You, Lord, that I have a legal title to the rights of the Son of God obtained by the judicial proceedings of the death and resurrection of Christ. I was adopted; the demands of this adoption were fulfilled by Christ's death on the cross.

Hallelujah! I am no longer a slave; I am free. I am His daughter, not because of my spirituality; my position in Christ makes me, legally and forensically.

Thank You, Jesus! Thank You for supernatural and unique privileges. Thank You for Your favor. The adversary had me, but God redeemed me. I am redeemed. Hallelujah! Hallelujah!

I am a legal child of God; a seed of Abraham, Isaac, and Jacob; adopted into the sonship; an heir of God through Christ; redeemed by the blood of the Lamb; a royal priesthood; a holy nation; God's treasured possession!

I have presented my case and my case laws. I give You thanks—how I thank You, Lord God! I have so much confidence in You, God. Show me who You are through this case. I am thanking You in advance for the victory.

You are able to do exceedingly, abundantly above all I could even ask or think. You are the Lord, the God of all flesh, and there is nothing too hard for You!

On the outside of the Courtroom, Sarah walked up and down.

Lord, I thank You that it is a fixed Court. This is a fixed case! This is a fixed Court. Thank You, Lord! Thank You, Jesus!

Ha, Satan, the devil, was just sitting out there; he is so upset because he knows there is a high chance that I will win the case because I appeared in Court. I showed up! I was late, but I showed up on time! I showed up, and I have my evidence! I confessed His Word in Court! I was functional in Court! There were no crocodile tears! I was not emotional … not acting religious! I was a legal, political kingdom–showing person.

Thank You, Lord! Thank You, Jesus! Show He who is God and God alone!

Meanwhile, the Righteous Judge is in His chambers, hearing every word that I say and smiling to Himself, saying, "That's My child; she is bragging on Me, expecting Me to give her a fair verdict. I can't let her down. I won't let her down. My promises are true and faithful."

God is not a man that He should lie, or the son of man that He should change His mind. Does He speak and not act? Does He promise and not fulfill (Numbers 23:19)?

Thank You, Jesus! Thank You, Lord! Glory to God! Hallelujah! Hallelujah! Hallelujah! Thank You, Lord! Thank You, Jesus!

The Verdict

THE RIGHTEOUS JUDGE, *while in His chambers*: Who is worshipping Me out there!

SARAH: Thank You, Jesus! Thank You, Lord! Lord, I den pay my tithes, yes, Lord! I den help ma neighbors, yes, Lord!

Father, You said to just say Your words and You will sort it out for me. Lord, You ask me, Your child, to come into Your chambers and You will give me Judge's privilege on behalf of my children and my children's children.
The Righteous Judge came out, pleased (smiling, proud of His child).

BAILIFF (Michael the Archangel): All rise! Order in His Court!

THE RIGHTEOUS JUDGE: Will the Accuser of the Brethren please stand. The Lord rebukes thee, O Satan; even the Lord that hath chosen Jerusalem rebukes thee. Is not this a brand plucked out of the fire?

As the Righteous Judge declares, "I hate robbery and wrong; I will faithfully give them their recompense" (Isaiah 61:8 ESV).
"[Satan] was a murderer from the beginning" (John 8:44) and he "comes only to steal and kill and destroy" (John 10:10 NIV).

People do not despise a thief if he steals to satisfy his hunger when he is starving. Yet if he is caught, he must pay sevenfold (full and complete compensation) though it costs him all the wealth of his house (Proverbs 6:30–31).

THE RIGHTEOUS JUDGE: Satan, Devil, Angel of Light, Lucifer, Accuser, Adversary, Deceiver, Liar, Thief, and Murderer—you have been found guilty on all counts. You are lawless and reckless. You have lawlessly lied, stolen, and murdered My child.

Sarah, I not only give you favor today, I will give you hidden treasures, riches stored in secret places, so that you may know that I am the Lord, the God of Israel, who summons you by name (Isaiah 45:3). And when you and your children return to the Lord your God and obey Him with all your heart and with all your soul according to everything I command you today, then the Lord your God will restore your fortunes and have compassion for you and gather you again from all the nations where He scattered you. Even if you have been banished to the most distant land under the heavens, from there the Lord your God will gather you and bring you back.

And to your request for that scholarship, I have already spoken to the minister. This time, you will not wait long to see him. You will have that audience with him. You will give him a copy of *Take Him to Court*.

Isaiah 14:15, 27: "… For the Lord of hosts hath purposed, and who shall disannul it? and his hand is stretched out, and who shall turn it back?"

All of a sudden, Sarah heard the crack of the gavel on the sound block.

This Court is adjourned! Next case, please! It's your time to take him to Court!

Your Things are in Storage Unclaimed

"Or again, how can anyone enter a strong man's house and carry off his possessions unless he first ties up the strong man? Then he can plunder his house" (Matthew 12:29 NIV).

- Your spiritual inheritance
- Your faith
- Your family
- Your production of good kids
- Your good health
- Your goals and dreams and success
- Financial blessings
- Your righteousness
- Your peace
- Your joy
- Psalm 119:162's promise

Tools of The Enemy

- Disappointment
- Despair
- Doubt
- Disbelief
- Distraction
- Deceit
- Double-mindedness
- Dishonesty
- Dullness
- Defilement
- Discontentment
- Delay
- Debt
- Disobedience

The Law: Ten Commandments

And God spoke all these words (Exodus 20).

1. I am the Lord your God, who brought you out of Egypt, out of the land of slavery.
2. You shall have no other gods before[a] me.
3. You shall not make for yourself an image in the form of anything in heaven above or on the earth beneath or in the waters below.
4. You shall not bow down to them or worship them; for I, the Lord your God, am a jealous God, punishing the children for the sin of the parents to the third and fourth generation of those who hate me.
5. Honor your father and your mother, so that you may live long in the land the Lord your God is giving you.
6. You shall not murder.
7. You shall not commit adultery.
8. You shall not steal.
9. You shall not give false testimony against your neighbor.
10. You shall not covet your neighbor's house. You shall not covet your neighbor's wife, or his male or female servant, his ox or donkey, or anything that belongs to your neighbor.

Accuser of The Brethren: Satan

The Accuser of the Brethren (Zechariah 3:1) is defending himself.

Satan's Profile:

- Is an adversary (Hebrew)
- Is a false accuser (Greek)
- Is a fallen angel who rebelled against God
- Is an enemy of God and man (a.k.a. power of darkness, prince of this world, tempter, god of this world, wicked one)
- Takes delight in accusing those who are saved and have been forgiven
- Corrupts the minds of believers (2 Corinthians 11:3)
- Steals the Word of God from the heart (Mark 4:15)
- Believes the most powerful tool is deceit (James 4:7; Revelation 12:9)

Cases Won

- My second Court appearance was in the Garden of Eden in Genesis 3. I won the case with Adam and Eve. I am so cunning, intelligent, and powerful that I was able to get Eve to trust in me rather than God—to doubt God's goodness. I got her to become discontented. I had her focus on the one thing she couldn't have and forget all the good things God had blessed her with in Eden.

- In the case of Judas Iscariot, I used my evil, wicked, proud, and cruel charm to get Judas to show an outward loyalty to Jesus. Deception! His heart was mine all along, he-he-he-he-he! That is why I was able to enter Judas according to Luke 22:48; he was a thief with greed in his heart. I got Judas to betray Jesus, you are no different. I got my eyes on you—yes, you!

Cases Lost

- My first Court appearance was in heaven. Did you know that I was the cherub that covereth; I was the one to protect God's throne? In Isaiah 14:12–14, I fell—no, I was kicked out of heaven because I wanted to be God. "How art thou fallen from heaven, O Lucifer, son of the morning! How art thou cut down to the ground, which didst weaken the nations! For thou hast said in thine heart, I will ascend into heaven, I will exalt my throne above the stars of God: I will sit also upon the mount of the congregation, in the sides of the north: I will ascend above the heights of the clouds; I will be like the most High." I wanted God's power and authority. My beauty and talent, riches and wisdom got the better of me, to my doom!

- I tempted the Apostle Peter so he would deny Christ, and he did, but Peter was restored by his Father.

- Job said, "Though he slay me yet will I trust Him." I couldn't win with Job. His mind was made up; he was sold out to God. No matter the test or trial, Job passed them all. Boy, if all Christians were like Job, my job would have been so hard.

But piece of cake—Christians do not know how to trust God. They strive on sight too much. Even I know the Word and I tremble by it.

- And last but not least, one of my most famous cases was with Jesus Christ the righteous. Now you know I have to be stupid to even try to tempt God! I did and lost big time (Matthew 4:1–11)!

Divine Defense Attorney: The Holy Spirit

The Holy Spirit's Profile:

- Relentless (Hebrews 7:25)
- He who helps our weaknesses (Romans 8:26)
- He who intercedes for us (Romans 8:26)
- Helper (John 14:16, 17, 26; 16:7)
- Advocate
- Lawyer (1 John 2:1)

The Holy Spirit's Qualities:

- The Spirit of judgment (Isaiah 4:4)
- The Spirit of wisdom and knowledge (Isaiah 11:2)
- The Spirit of grace and supplication (Zechariah 12:10)
- The Comforter (John 14:26)
- The Spirit of truth (John 14:17, 15:26)
- The Spirit of counsel and might (Acts 1:8, 8:29, 16:6–7)

Cases Won / Cases Lost

He has never lost a case; his Father is the Righteous Judge.

God, The Righteous Judge Presiding

God's Profile:

- Omnipotent (all-powerful)
- Omniscient (all-knowing)
- Omnipresent (everywhere)
- Creator of the universe
- God the Father, the Supreme Being
- I AM THAT I AM
- First and Last
- Elohim
- Adonai
- El Shaddai
- Holy and just

About The Author

A twin and the ninth of eleven children, Sarah Jane Mackey was born and raised in Moss Town, on the island of Exuma in the Bahamas. She resides in New Providence with her husband Sidney. They have five children.

As a child, she was adventurous: climbing trees, building her own birdcage and scooter, and making dolls out of straw, among other things, but her first love was reading.

Sarah loves gardening. The planting, weeding, sowing, pruning, and lawn were the building blocks that have taught her many important life lessons.

Though she has had many struggles along the way, the lessons learned made her strong and resilient. "Bad ain't bad" she would say, and or "Less is more" because she submitted to the lesson remembering that, "In everything give God thanks".

Sarah's passion is encouraging others: the lost or saved; rich or poor; learned or unlearned; happy or sad. She listens with her eyes, hears with her hands, and speaks life into the ear of her listeners.

Today, her message is clear, "take him to Court." If you think someone has stolen your authority in God, and you are having a hard time exercising complete trust in Him, wake up! Someone is squatting on your land and living there for free, robbing you and your later generations of your inheritance. It's time to go to Court for it.

Sarah has been writing since 1998.

In 2014, she wrote her first book of poems, *Under Pressure: Poems of Deliverance.*

In 2021, she wrote, *Under Pressure: Poems of Deliverance Book 2*

In 2021 she wrote, *Under Pressure Puzzles*

Printed in the United States
by Baker & Taylor Publisher Services